Poems to God

Written by Amy Boatright Illustrated by Kim Sponaugle

This book is dedicated to my three beautiful children whose lives inspired me to write these poems while they were just toddlers and to my sweet Grandma Becky whose last conversation with me included the question, "Have you finished your book?" - Amy Boatright

ISBN- 978-1-0879-3106-7

Design and Layout by Rosemarie Gillen

Printed in the U.S.A.

Table of Contents

Good Morning Lord

Good morning, Lord, and thank You,
For You blessed me through the night.
And when I couldn't get to sleep,
You helped me through my fright.

Good morning, Lord, and thank You,
For I know You'll bless my day.
And bring me joy in all I do,
Keep me safe in every way.

Good morning, Lord, and thank You,
Help me to work as hard as I can.
To make You super proud of me,
As I fulfill Your plan.

Good morning, Lord, and thank You,
For each of Your creations.
I hope that You'll shine through me today,
And keep me from temptation.

Amen

My Temptation Prayer

Dear Lord, why is it easier sometimes,
To do wrong instead of right?
Why does the darkness seem,
More inviting than the light?

Deep down in my heart,
I want to do what's good.
God, please make me strong enough,
To do the things I should.

Sometimes my friends do wrong,
I just seem to do it, too.
I do it without thinking first,
Without thinking about You.

God, please write me down,
On Your list of "need to dos."
So when I have a chance,
It will be easier to choose.

Dear Lord, my heart feels warm and fuzzy,
Knowing You never leave me alone.
To attempt to be tough enough,
To resist what You don't condone!

Amen

My Forgiveness Prayer

Dear Lord, no one's perfect,
So I know that I have sins.
I've heard that You'll forgive me,
Like You have all other men.

There are times I know I'm sinning,
When I can see something's not Your way.
Other times I may be sinning,
And just think everything's okay!

Regardless of my intentions,
I've done wrong and I feel sad.
God, will you please forgive me,
And wipe away the bad?

Thank You, God, for Your forgiveness,
I will pray this every day.
I ask for You to cleanse me,
In Jesus' name I pray.

Amen

MOLLIE'S
TOYS

My Playtime Prayer

All right, God, we need to talk,
I'm having a rough day.
See, sometimes I'm kind of stingy,
So nobody wants to play.

God, I need Your assistance,
Can You teach me to share my toys?
Because it's really not much fun,
To fight with other girls and boys.

And God, I would be so grateful,
If You would help us get along.
And help me to shut my mouth,
When my attitude is wrong.

Please help me when other kids tease me,
To remember two wrongs don't make a right!
Even if my heart feels sad,
Help me to shine Your light!

Now last, just wipe my tears away,
Because they call me a baby when I cry.
Well, can you do all this for me?
I thought so, thanks, Big Guy!

Amen

My Mealtime Prayer

It's me again, God,
Can You do me a favor?
You see it's mealtime right now,
And my veggies lost their flavor.

I've tried holding my nose,
And every other little trick.
Lord, can You help me shove them down,
And can You do it kind of quick?

Don't get me wrong, God,
Thank You for my food.
I really do appreciate it,
I don't mean to sound so rude.

God, my mommy told me,
"You can't get up until they're gone."
Please help them to taste better,
So I won't be here all night long!

I know that they are good for me,
And I'm sure they'll help me grow.
But it's hard for me to fork them down,
In spite of what I know.

Okay, God, here I go,
I'm gonna make my mommy glad.
First bite, here goes nothing.....
Hey! That's not so bad!

What do you know,
You did it again.
Thank You, dear God,
You're such a good friend!

Amen

My Blessing

God, I'd like to make this short and sweet,
Thank You for this food to eat.
Please bless it to my nourishment,
And make my mealtime, well spent.
Thank You for three meals a day,
Thank You, Lord, in every way.

Amen

MY BATH TIME PRAYER

RUB-A-DUB-DUB, DEAR GOD, I'M IN THE TUB,
CAN YOU MAKE ME SHINY AS A DIME?
AND HELP ME WIPE AWAY THE EVIDENCE,
FROM EVERY TREE THAT I HAVE CLIMBED?

GOODNESS, I PLAYED REAL HARD TODAY,
SO I'M GONNA ASK YOU FROM THE START.
WITHOUT A DOUBT, COULD YOU HELP ME OUT,
AND CLEAN MY EVERY LITTLE BODY PART?

LORD, KEEP ME UNDER CONTROL,
BECAUSE MOMMY'S FROWN LOOKS KIND OF STUCK!
WHEN I LEAVE HER A MESS, FROM THE TIME I UNDRESS,
SHE SAYS, "LITTLE ONE! BATH TIME'S UP!"

LORD, THANK YOU FOR MY RUBBER DUCKY,
AND EACH BOAT AND DOLL AND TOY.
BECAUSE IF I DIDN'T HAVE THESE BLESSINGS,
BATH TIME WOULDN'T BE SUCH A JOY.

DEAR GOD, YOU SURE ARE SMART,
AND IF IT WASN'T FOR EVERYTHING YOU KNOW.
THERE WOULD BE NO SUCH THING AS BATH TIME,
AND I WOULD BE STINKY FROM HEAD TO TOE!

AMEN

God, Help The Hurting Children

God, there are children,
Who have problems in their homes.
Things don't feel secure for them,
And they often feel alone.

I know that Your word tells us,
A friend loves at all times.
But I'm not exactly sure,
How to help these friends of mine.

So I ask for You to give them,
A great big heavenly hug!
Help them to know they aren't alone,
And please let them know they're loved!

It's really hard to understand,
Why bad things happen on this earth.
But no matter what the bad may be,
It never changes our worth!

If we know You as our Savior,
We will always have a friend.
And what ever we may go through,
You'll be with us 'til the end.

Amen

My Holiday Prayer

There are few holidays, Lord,
That could be here without You.
Help us not forget You, God,
When we're in the festive mood.

On New Year's Day help us remember,
That You've allowed us another year.
At Valentine's there would be no hearts,
Without Your love, so dear!

There would be no Easter baskets,
If You hadn't risen from the dead.
At fall festivals, no mask,
If You hadn't blessed us with our heads.

Thanksgiving would be thankless,
But for Your gift of friends.
And Christmas gifts, forget it,
If Baby Jesus wasn't sent.

Jesus, we are really blessed,
From all Your jolly ways.
Help us to remember that,
On every holiday.

Amen

God, For You

Dear God, I often ask,
For me what You can do.
While failing to remember,
What I should do for You.

Lord, I'm gonna to tell the world,
About Your loving heart!
Let them know that You are here,
And have been from the start!

I'll make sure to tell them,
That You will forgive.
And that You will love them,
No matter how they've lived.

And, God, I'll be glad to tell them,
You'll be coming back one day.
Dear God, I'll tell them anything!
Just show me what to say.

Dear God, You've been so good to me,
I just can't keep it all inside!
I want the whole world to know,
In You they can confide!

Amen

GONE FISHIN'
POP POP

My Grief Prayer

God, my heart is hurting,
For someone I love is gone.
I'm sad because I'm missing them,
It's hard to pretend I'm strong.

I'm thankful that when I talk with You,
I don't have to pretend.
I can tell You how I really feel,
You are such a loving friend.

Will You please mend my heart?
Sometimes I just want to cry.
And though I know You are in charge,
It's okay to wonder why!

As I live my life each day,
It doesn't mean I forgot or it's not sad.
Please help me to try to choose joy,
When I'm beginning to dwell on the bad.

This will be very hard for me,
So, as this prayer comes to an end.
I ask You to give me the strength I need,
In Jesus' name, Amen!

My Bedtime Prayer

It's time for me to go to sleep,
Lord, while I'm in the bed.
I pray that You will bless me,
With angels 'round my head.

I know that I will dream tonight,
So, God, will You be sure.
To make each one so heavenly,
All soft and sweet and pure.

And, God, I need forgiveness,
For what I was unaware.
So when I wake in the morn,
Your grace, with others I'll share.

Please bless every single person,
Who has a place in my heart.
I'm sure I don't have to name them, God,
Because I know You're really smart.

I think that's everything,
Uh huh, I got it right.
My eyes are getting heavy now,
Okay, dear God, good night.

Amen

The Tale of Why God Made Little Kids: A Life Lesson

In your life you may hear many tales that are cute,
But you must always remember there is only one Truth.
So just ask God to give you His mighty insight,
And He'll show you when something just isn't right!

For example, this tale of how kids came about,
An adorable story that you would never doubt.
But let us learn a life lesson as we read below,
It goes something like this, here we go:

After God made the beautiful rivers,
And after He said, "Let there be light."
He realized that He needed more,
He wanted joy with all His might.

He wanted some kind of joyful creature,
He wanted some kind of joyful noise.
He wanted someone to play with His latest creation,
He wanted someone to play with His new toys!

So He challenged Himself and with effortless thought,
He came up with the perfect way.
He said, "I'll make a person, a tiny one,
And I think I'll make them today!"

First He made one kind with cute little legs,
And made sure of her pretty curls.
Then thought and thought to come up with a name,
He called them His little girls.

Now the second kind was a little odd,
Sort of stocky and rough with his toys.
And while watching him play, He decided one day,
He would call them His little boys.

Then He looked upon the earth,
At all the work that He did.
And He called out proudly,
"My world is complete! I've got my little kids!"

Now wasn't that story just super cute?
You could hardly tell that it isn't the truth!
That is the lesson for you to learn from this,
Pay close attention so nothing is missed!

You see, the Bible shows that this tale isn't true,
That God really thought so much more of you.
That He made you earthy parents first,
He picked them to care for you before birth.

It actually all started,
When He made Adam and Eve.
The first people on this earth,
With His dynamite speed!

So to see if something measures up,
You must put what you hear to the test.
Just because something sounds good,
Doesn't always mean it's best!

The End

Amy Boatright is a wife, mother of three, Maymee to a precious little granddaughter, and healthcare worker from Savannah, Ga.

She is also a pet mommy to a very spoiled golden retriever and a sweet tuxedo kitty cat. She enjoys having her family together and feeding them until they are stuffed. She is a lifetime student of God's perfect love and forgiveness.

There aren't many things that she loves as much as coffee, except maybe chocolate, a day on the beach, or a beautiful hike in the North Georgia Mountains. Her hobbies include singing, running, coaching, cooking, and laughing. But her greatest passions are creative writing and pouring into the lives of those God brings across her path!

CPSIA information can be obtained
at www.ICGtesting.com
Printed in the USA
LVHW070535231220
674886LV00010B/936

9 781087 931067